Content Warnings: Suicidal ideation, verbal abuse, arraigned marriage, mentions of murder and poisoning

BENEATH THE SILVERN POND
M.A BROWN
A PENNIES WORTH OF
DREAD NOVELLA

Cover Art/Title Page/Chapter Headers: By Giulia Martini @julsiji Interior Full-Page Illustration: By @koijix

Beta Readers: Cynthia Brubaker, Jenn Trocine, Stephanie Combs, Heather Reynolds

Dev editor: Beth Steadman Copy/Line editor: EFC Editing Services

Contents

CHAPTER ONE

The percussion of the raindrops on the lily pads was what first drew me to the pond on the far side of Grandon Manor. Something about the luring tones had given my longing ears the impression of a singer. Someone must have given those notes voice, and yet there was nothing there but me and the lilies.

I sloshed my way to the lip of the silvern pond through the verdant verge in my bare feet and dressing gown. Tucking myself into a hollow made of bent reeds and bowed hemlock, I curled up on a flat stone with my feet pulled under my hem and wallowed. I kept my head cocked and my ear bent to listen to the vastly lonesome sound of the fat drops of rain as they met their end against the fragrant greenery before they rolled off leaves and bled into the seemingly depthless pond. My heartbeats synced to the sound like a pianist keeping time with a metronome. My breaths slowed. I could almost imagine that if I stayed this way long enough that I might begin to grow moss. My skin might become stone, and I would cease to feel anything other than the gentle stroking of the shallows against my soul.

But that dream could never be. I was to marry, and I was to marry rich. For all our sakes.

"Lucrecia? Lucrecia?" The concerned calls of my grandmother, dampened by the swirl of mist, pulled me out of my trance, and I poked my head out from my haven.

"I am here, Grandam," I reluctantly replied.

The old crone shrieked when she laid eyes on me, the fog robbing the sound of most of its potency. "Lucrecia, come away from there!" She flailed her sagging arms frantically from where she'd stopped, paces away from the edge of the liquid abyss. "The waters are cursed, come away from them now."

She held out her hand, her fingers trembling like the feathers on the broken wing of a dead bird, and in that moment, I pitied her.

"I think if you come have a look, Grandam, you would see how lovely it is here. Come and sit a spell before we go in." What I didn't dare voice was that I was not yet ready to be fussed over and preened so I could be presented to yet more suitors. Each had been worse than the last, and each had made a bit more of my heart wither every passing day.

Grandmother paled, her complexion made as waxy as a wriggling maggot's flesh as it worked its way through cheese. She shook her head, and her damp curls, more salt than pepper, stuck to her cheeks. "I wouldn't dare. The pond is a portal to the realm of the *sidhe*. The fairies, one might drag me in and drown me."

I looked over the gray water, curiosity stretched out like a net, as though I could catch a glimpse of a sidhe just by knowing one might reside there.

"Lucrecia, please," my grandmother begged yet again. Her words threatened tears soon to follow, so I relented. But as I stood, a ripple caught my eye, there and then gone again as if the rain covered the movement. A chill slid down my spine like the slip of a snail, and I couldn't stop my bones from shivering. The whole way back to the house, my arm linked with the old woman's, I could not help but swivel my head round every pace or so to see if I could spy again the strange motion, nor could I shake the notion that something watched me.

Mother always insisted on bathing me in buttermilk and flowers. Fragmented petals of calendula, chamomile, and rose stuck to my skin as I soaked in the warmth and let it all wash away the smell of the muddied murk that clung to my flesh from my early outing to the pond. I resented the fragrance for stealing from me that little memory of stolen freedom as my grandmother struggled to pull a tortoiseshell comb through the matted tangles of my pale hair with arthritic fingers, freeing trapped hemlock blossoms from the locks.

"You're not dressed yet." My mother hurled the words at me, rife with accusation and disgust as she bustled into the room and ripped the curtains open. A host of skittish maids, borrowed from a neighboring household, scurried at her heels, carting boxes and yards of fabric draped over their arms like scared little mice tiptoeing around a hungry cat.

I sank lower into the opaque waters until everything but my nose and eyes were completely submerged. There was no point in replying to her, as she never heard words that she didn't wish to, no matter how logical or impassioned they may be. Her selective deafness, despite its inconveniences, was one of the things I admired most about the woman who'd given birth to me. It meant she simply didn't hear the scathing things said about our family. Rumors couldn't touch her, so her shoulders never stooped under the same shame as mine did as socialites' little comments bit me like the late summer flies. I admired that and her hair. She and I shared the same soft golden color, but she'd never cut hers a day in her life. It fell in such long waves that when unbound, it cascaded behind her like a bridal train.

Today, she had it in a series of braids, with pins carved to look like all manner of butterflies fixing some of the long ropes to the top of her head in a mass of elaborate coils while the rest hung free. She looked like an exotic flower. If only her disposition were as such. She peered at me, a perturbed wrinkle to her nose as she looked me over more thoroughly, from the muck beneath my nails to the greenery in my snarled locks. "Are you trying to irk me with your appearance, or are you just inept?"

A maid came running in from the corridor, saving me from having to answer. Her cheeks were flushed as she skidded to a stop next to my mother. "My Lady Sinella," the harried woman huffed, her color only deepened as my mother rounded on her and fixed her with a lioness's glare. "I was sent to fetch you. The prospective matches for Lady Lucrecia are starting to arrive."

"Do you think me a fool?" Mother arched a slimly plucked pale brow at the poor thing whose lip began to quiver.

"I—well—I," the unfortunate servant stammered. I pitied her. I'd been on the other side of that look more times than I cared to be, and I was sure that I would be again sooner rather than later.

"Do you think I am unaware of what is going on in this house? Do you think I missed the fact that there is a gaggle of men with deep pockets lining up to inspect my daughter's charms? Or that you spent the night rolling in the barn loft with some stable hand judging from the hay matted into the scraggly strands of your ghastly hair?"

Tears began to well in the woman's eyes, but my mother would not be stopped. Unable to bear hearing any more of the wild and cutting words that she slung at the unnerved woman, I slid beneath the milky murk, submerging my whole head until all her words were garbled like the song of bullfrogs. I imagined this must have been what it was like to sink into the silvery pond.

The musicians moved like nervous grasshoppers wary of a bird venturing too close as they dragged bows across their stringed instruments in the greater ballroom of my grandmother's estate. The result was a sharp edge to their otherwise jovial tune that made me want to grind my teeth.

Opulence was the name of tonight's game. Despite the fact that we as a family had nothing but cobwebs in our coffers, we couldn't dare make that obvious to my prospective suitors and risk them running away. So instead of modest negotiations and meetings done quietly over tea, we were all forced into this garish societal dance paid for with the credit that came with my grandmother's good name. Coiled silver ribbons twirled from the ceiling, some fluttered in the sweet breeze coming from the windows flung wide along

the far wall, while others held carefully crafted orbs of white and blue flora.
If you squinted closely, you could see
the curl on the petals. If you breathed
deeply, you could smell the subtle
decay of several day-old foliage that
hinted at the state of our coin purses.
Even the rope of pearls looped round
and round my neck like a noose were
painted plaster.

Servants mingled, dressed in the
family colors of indigo and ivory,
and offered silver chalices of wa-
tered-down mulberry wine to the riot
of bachelors. The only women in attendance other than myself were already married or spinsters too old
to be considered competition by my
mother's view, but as all eyes turned
to us as we finally stepped across the

threshold, I silently wished that every hot-blooded male there would suddenly take an interest in the older women rather than myself.

Dozens of eyes peeled my flesh, dissecting me, stripping me bare. I was a flower pressed into glass admired for my beauty and not my worth. I was something to behold but never to be loved. Someone announced us, but the words were a scream tearing through one ear before raging out the other. My stays squeezed like a giant's fist around my rib cage, determined to make me into jelly. My stocking ribbons constricted like slithering snakes, and heat spilled violently across my cheeks.

Mother took me by the elbow—her touch, I'm sure, was outwardly tender—but the truth of it was that it had teeth. Each of her nails pressed into my skin so firmly as she dragged me across the floor that I could feel the purple of bruises forming. Father followed uselessly on her other side, her stoop-shouldered shadow.

"Ah, Lord Fortescue." My mother's mask of sweetness and charm slipped over her viperous face as a tall graying gentleman cut across our path and bowed. He was easily old enough to be my grandfather, who'd been long in the grave, but he had gold and diamond rings on his fingers, and so that was, I'm sure, all my mother cared about.

"My lady Sinella, it is—" He pressed a handkerchief to his lips, and coughed, the sound wet and hacking leaving a waft of coppery tang in the space between us, before he could continue. "What a lovely event you have put on this evening. And this must be the Lady Lucrecia?" He peered down his long nose at me, his watery eyes hungry.

I curtsied as I was supposed to and fluttered my lashes demurely, before softly saying, "It is a pleasure to meet you, my lord." It was anything but, and my skin crawled at the lie.

"My, my, she is a willowy slip of a thing," the lord commented, though it wasn't immediately clear whether he meant it as a compliment or not. "Are those hips of hers wide enough to bear sons do you think?" Not a compliment then.

"She is more than capable, I assure you." My mother snapped her fan open and bellowed it in front of her as she replied with her voice pitched loud enough for those dropping eaves to hear. "We had as much confirmed by a midwife."

Hushed mutterings of approval and appreciation swept through the nearest gathered men like the murmuring of cicadas at sundown. Embarrassment flushed through my body like a brush fire, and I hid my flaming cheeks behind the flutter of my own fan.

The night devolved from there. I was put through my paces like a prize pony at show. With hundreds of eyes stuck to me like flies in honey, I demonstrated my mastery of the violin, watercolor, and embroidery until my fingers threatened to bleed at stations set up around the room with ample supplies for my exhibitions. As if my display of talents was not enough, I was then led by every man in attendance in at least one dance apiece.

My gaze kept lingering past the sills of the windows to the hazy, distant glimmer of moonlight on the water. It beckoned me like a spider summoning a fly to its web. I would have gladly drowned in its depths over being trapped here.

An ill wind swept in, stirring the curtains, and sent rumpled flower petals raining from the carefully curated décor as the doors to the ballroom banged open.

"Announcing Lord Tursel of Eaton." The borrowed herald's voice rang sonorously over the assembled suitors.

The crowd parted around the newcomer like minnows making way for a larger fish in a small pond. And he was indeed a larger fish, if the preening my mother did as she set eyes upon him was any indication. Even Father straightened and looked up from his wine cup.

He swept in like a thunderstorm over the rolling hills. His hair and eyes were dark as they locked hungrily on mine. He was younger by half than all the other suitors in the room, with a smooth-cut jaw that did not sag in the jowls, nor was there any hint of age in his locks. But there was something in the curl of his smile as he bent low over my hand that made the blood in my veins run cold.

"Lord Tursel, a pleasure to see you," my mother fawned. "I didn't know if you would receive our invitation seeing as your wife passed so recently, and so tragically too."

The lord took her hand in turn, bowing low over it. Each of his movements seemed to have a flourish, like a well-rehearsed dance. "Ah yes, well, I admit, the ache of a cold marital bed has been chafing as of late, and the prospect of being introduced to such a delicate flower stirred me from my grief." His voice was velvety, but it slithered over me like an adder in the grass, and my spine went rigid.

My father coughed, his face broken and purpled from years of too much drink. "Tursel, good to see you again, son. I was sorry to hear of your father's passing, but understand that your gentleman's club is flourishing now that you've inherited it, so I suppose congratulations are also in order."

A slimy smile split the man's face. "Thank you, my lord, and you, sir, of course, are more than welcome to come visit on credit—"

"No, no, I couldn't. Gambling is such a nasty habit. I never touch it." If only that sentiment were true. My father had made a series of poor investments, which was the high society term for squandering all your money on gambling and houses of ill repute.

Grandmother had paid off the enormous sums he'd owed to keep him out of debtors' prison and our family name off the lips of gossips, but it had sucked her bank accounts dry, leaving nothing but a brittle hollow space where wealth and prominence had once been. And the gossips still flocked to the scandal like vultures to a day-old carcass.

"Of course." Tursel cut my father off smoothly and turned his attention back to me. "Might I have a dance, Lady Lucrecia?"

I was loath to accept, especially when my too-small slippers pinched and a riot of blisters were screaming beneath my stockings. But my mother answered for me, "Of course, she will!" She shoved me forward into his arms and began frantically signaling to the musicians to change their tempo. There was a screech of strings before they found themselves again and settled into a melody that was neither fast nor slow.

The dance floor cleared, leaving Tursel and me alone. His hand felt heavy on my hip and his fingers crushing as he pulled me along, a firm lead. The nauseating scent of gardenia wafted off him, but beneath the thick layer of floral was the smell of something sinister that made me think of the metallic tang of dried blood. It reminded me that he was not only a widower, but he had also recently lost his father. It was as if death clung to him, like the shrouds that no doubt clung to his loved ones' waxen and drawn post-mortem flesh. I swallowed hard, a notion flitting through the most shadowy recesses of my mind. What if their deaths had not been natural? Mother always did chastise me for what she called my fits of fancy, outlandish notions that popped into my head plucked from the ether or imagination. Grandmother, on the other hand, called it my intuition. She said the knowing of unsaid things ran thickly in our blood and that the whispering from our subconscious should never be ignored.

Unable to keep my tongue still, I found myself asking, "How is it that your wife passed, my lord?"

He chuckled, though the sound echoed hollowly. "Such an impertinent question for a lady. Have you asked such crass things of all your widowed suitors this evening?"

I didn't answer as he twirled me around, the faces of the other attendees blurring and bleeding like a painting left in the rain. Any words I thought to speak to defend my bluntness immediately became choked like fish bones in my throat.

Tursel leaned in, humming against my temple. "Never you mind what happened to my late wife. It is no matter when you'll be my next."

That notion loosened my tongue. "But you haven't asked. I haven't accepted."

The laugh that he let out this time was not a fake one. No, this time he tipped his chin back and threw the full and throaty sound to the gods. "The grape on the vine does not get to decide when it is plucked, sweet one. That is up to the vintner. But—mmmm—" He breathed in deeply, running his nose inappropriately along the curve of my neck, no doubt inhaling the lingering milk and petals from my bath, but no one stopped him or called him a cad for his lewdness. "I can't wait to taste you on my tongue."

I shuddered deep in my marrow and shut my eyes against the tears that nettled at the back of my eyelids.

With deft hands, he spun me round and pressed my back against his chest. Something coolly metallic slipped like a garrote around my neck.

"A token of my intentions," he hissed in my ear as the music crescendoed.

We turned to face one another as the singing of the strings ended, giving one another the proper bow and curtsy due. Applause littered the room, sweeping like a scattering of leaves in a breeze around the vast space. I ran my fingers over the pendant he'd hung around my neck, his claiming mark. A delicate filigree orb.

My mother and father rushed to my side. Their eager chatter may as well have been a murderous cawing of crows for all of it I heard over the ringing in my ears until one word struck through: "Betrothed."

CHAPTER
TWO

With a scream half stolen by the mists, I tossed the grotesque and garish golden trinket into the pond and collapsed onto the stone in the little hollow of hemlock. I drew my knees up to my chest and buried my face into my skirts with a sob. I could not marry that man, and yet the fact remained that I had no say in the matter. Ignatius Tursel had the largest annual income and the deepest family vaults. He, as he'd so eloquently put it while sequestered in a private parlor after the ball's end, would pay any sum to my father for an unspoiled bride, and he had the coffers to do it.

A soft splash and an odd plinking drew a sharp gasp from my lips as I jolted my head up to see if I'd been discovered yet again by my grandmother or, worse, by my intended. I could see nothing but the long expanse of rippling pond, quicksilver in the moonlight. But then I felt a cool brush along my bare foot. With wide eyes, I looked down to find the golden orb pendant somehow returned to me.

Curiously, I plucked it and rolled the detestable thing between my fingers. "How in the gods?" I whispered. Was someone there with me? I called out and received no reply but the gentle lapping of the waters. Was it cursed? Not everyone held to the belief that objects could bear people ill, but having grown up so close to the dark wood, I'd heard the tales of witches that lived in their depths that would cast the most preposterous of spells and incantations, for a price of course. There were even legends that the moon itself was a woman who'd made such a bargain. I peered up at it, squinting to see if I could spot any sort of feminine features in the curve of the luminescent sphere, but from the height at which it sat, I could only imagine.

There could only be one way to tell for certain if the bauble was bad, and that was to persist in ridding myself of it. At least, that was what I'd gleaned from the tales—objects of such dark natures would always find their way back to you no matter how you toiled to be free of them. I sucked in a breath, letting it fill my lungs to the brim, and tossed the trinket back into the silvern depths.

I watched in silence, the thrum of my heart beating in time to the drone of the frogs and the song of the grasshoppers, melding me into a pond creature the same as them. I waited long enough that my nerves were soothed and my anxieties as-suaged. But then, out of the corner of my eye, I saw the pad of a lily ruffle. And with a chink of metal on stone, the pendant dropped in front of me once more.

No longer was I a part of the beauty of the ecosystem in which I sat, but I was very, painfully separate. My pulse surged through me, sending the bells of alarm in the back of my mind ringing. Had Tursel bewitched the bauble? And if so, to what end? But perhaps this was all another flight of fancy, my mind running away with itself yet again. Mayhap there simply was someone here with me as I'd first thought and this was some childish jape meant to scare me.

"Who's there?" I called out on a tenuous breath.

For a long pause, there was nothing, no response, and I thought in the stillness that I'd succumbed to some sort of temporary madness, but then I remembered my grandmother's fear from the morning. It bled into me, and I made it my own. Perhaps I ought to have listened to her, maybe I should not have strayed. A lily shifted, drifting across the waters of its own will, and I gasped as it slowly began to rise.

It took a thunderingly anxious moment for me to realize that the flower did not simply levitate on its own, but that there was something attached to its underside. I let my gaze drip slowly down. The creature had red hair, but not the red of an apple. No, this was the red of muddied blood. It had skin that looked silken and dewy, and green. It's eyes fixed on mine were moony, bulbous, and black. But they were startlingly entrapping, bizarre and sumptuous, and I found that I could not tear my gaze away from where they sank just below the surface. It rose a fraction more, as though it were more wary of me than I was of it, and exposed delicate and humanoid cheekbones, followed by a languid swanlike neck, collarbones, and then a pair of heavy breasts with nipples peaked against the chill water.

It—she—trilled and nodded toward the golden pendant still in my palm. Dumbstruck, I looked down at it and then back up at her. "You brought this back to me." My words were thin, drawn out by my awe.

She smiled, and it sent a shiver through my marrow that was not altogether fearful even though I suspected it should have been. Her teeth were jagged points, in neat rows like pearls on a string, and I was struck with the oddest desire to run my tongue over them and found myself running it over my own blunt ivory gnashers with a disappointed air.

"Thank you." I uncurled myself and slid tentatively toward the edge of my rock. She watched me, unmoving, her infinitely dark eyes marking every movement as I dipped a toe into the cool water and then let first one foot sink into the depths and then the other until the gentle lap of the pond caressed the backs of my knees. I held my hand outstretched, the ball-shaped filigree pendant cradled in the heart of my palm like an egg in the nest—an offering. "Would you like to keep it?"

A trilling sound, not unlike the one that had drawn me to this very spot through the morning mists, vibrated in her throat. In a rush of jerky waters, she swished forward, her eyes fixed on my hand. Her arm rose from the water, trailing with it ribbons of aquatic weed. Her fingers were long with delicate webbing strung between them at the base, like an intricate twist of lace. She wrapped them around my forearm and trailed them slowly down the exposed skin. I felt her moist touch like a swarm of lightning bugs through my whole body, illuminating and fluttering in places so deep and dark within me I didn't even know they existed. A whimper fell through my parted lips, and I bit them to keep any more of the taste of that surprisingly pleasurable sound from escaping. With deft movements, she plucked the orb up and pressed it to her cheek and nuzzled against the bright metal. "Thank you, the sidhe do not forget a gift so freely given." Her voice was melodic, like a sliver of rainbow kissing the surface of the waters during a raging storm.

It was only when she chuckled and leaned in to brush her fingers along my jaw that I realized my mouth hung open. "You can speak?" My words seemed to delight her, and something akin to mirth flashed in her deep eyes.

"I can speak, child of the mud and stone, same as you. Though I rarely speak your tongue." *Tongue*—oh gods, why did she have to mention tongues? My gaze fell to her mouth where I caught a hint of pink flesh darting behind her lips, and my mind strayed again to running mine along those teeth, and I couldn't help but wonder if she would want to try tasting me as well.

Hypnotically, I leaned forward, my hands pressed against the stone beneath me so I could lever myself into her space, just a little bit more, so I could fill my nostrils with her scent—all green and floral and moss. "Do you have a name, sidhe?" I asked mesmerically. I had to have it to carry with me.

She canted her head to the side and examined me, her eyes roving along my edges as if trying to determine my worth. Though with her, the assessment did not chafe as it did in that

stifling ballroom under the scrutiniz-
ing glowers of the men who thought
to purchase me. "Is that the price you
demand for the pretty?" She held the
pendant between us to indicate what
she meant.

I shook my head, and my hair tum-
bled free from its final restraint to
spill over my shoulders. "No, I don't
want payment. That was a gift. I just
want to know your name so we can
be—" I flushed, my blood rushing to
my cheeks heatedly. What did I want
us to be? What could a sidhe and a
human be? "Friends," I settled on. "I
would like us to be friends."

The waters of the pond rushed over
the stone, saturating my bunched
skirts and flooding my seat as she
swam close enough that her breasts

pressed against the knobs of my knees. She placed a gentle hand to my cheek, and I could feel every point of contact with such stark clarity that it rooted me to the spot as still as the granite below me. I feared moving might prompt her to pull away from my suddenly too-heated flesh, and I didn't want to have to experience the loss.

She rose up until we were eye to eye. "Ilona is what you may call me, mud girl. You may have it as a gift." She crooned her words softly, leaning in and whispering them against my ear so that I knew they were only for me. Her hair dripped, and the chill of it rolled down my collarbone, slid over its prominence, leaving a trail of gooseflesh as it made its way between my breasts.

I turned my head just a fraction, angling it so I could whisper against her pointed mossy green ear, "I'm called Lucrecia." I could have sworn I felt a tremor run through her slick body before she withdrew, sinking back into the pond leaving me gasping and aching for her touch.

"I will see you again soon I hope, Lucrecia, lady of the mud." And then she was gone with nothing but a wayward lily adrift across the ripples she'd left in her wake.

"You're not wearing your necklace?" My suitor had teeth. Not like hers. Not where I could see them, but I could still feel them devouring my flesh in his imagination, so clearly lecherous behind those hooded dark eyes and that too-charismatic smile that said, *"Look here but look no further, you wouldn't like what's in my depths."*

As I sipped my tea, my gaze drifted over the rim, through the window and down the hill where Ilona's pond lay puddled like spilled quicksilver among the reeds and other greenery that thrashed in the early summer's breeze. The shadows of the nearby woods curled like a lover's fingers among the grasses and caressed the lip of the water. Wistfully, I wondered what it would be like to have my skin in her teeth, my fingernails dragging across her flesh and through her hair.

The shrill chink of a cup upon a saucer snapped my gaze back to those sitting at the table. My mother glared at me, her cheeks flamed apoplectically. "My dear, Ignatius asked you a question."

I blinked at him slowly, my senses hazed with the longing to be anywhere but there. "My apologies, Lord Tursel. What was it you asked?"

His eyes narrowed as he rasped, "Your necklace, where is it?"

"I was unaware I was to keep it on at all times like a dog does a collar." The reply, so daring and unladylike, rolled off my tongue like dew from a leaf without thought.

My father sputtered from his half-inebriated stupor. A spray of biscuit crumbs hailed down from his aghast, choking mouth. Mother dropped her cup, the fine porcelain, painted in a lilac floral pattern, shattering against the lace-covered table. But Tursel . . . he remained as poised as a ballerina performing one of the midsummer romances. And that was probably the most unnerving thing of all. He had the same wicked glint in his eye that I'd seen only once before when I was small and our stableman managed to trap and drag a unicorn filly from the depths of the dark wood to be broken. The poor thing had cried for days under his ministrations until at long last she succumbed to his demands. But in doing so, she lost her luminous periwinkle luster, her horn rotted off, and everything that made her unique and beautiful was gone. I was no rarity like she'd been, but a fear twisted in my gut as he and I locked eyes in a clashing stare, and I suddenly knew that if I were to become his wife, I'd soon be in a muddied hole like his first wife and his father.

Excuses for my behavior were shrilly pitched and volleyed from both my parents between screeches to summon a servant to clean up the mess I'd made with my rudeness and demands that my grandmother hurry me away for a nap. Ignatius's eyes never left me. I could feel them on me like the unyielding chill of a mausoleum long after Grandam whisked me into my chamber. She locked me in with the rasp of a key, no doubt on my mother's orders. She was not so innately cruel as to think to do such a thing herself, and I could not begrudge her for it.

I shivered uncontrollably as I paced before my bedroom window, constantly aware of the silvery waters in my periphery until darkness fell. The tapers in my room remained unlit, and my belly began to crawl with hunger. But I knew I would be left with neither light nor food. This punishment was one I knew by rote, a favored of my mother's. The only question was for how long would it last? A day, two, ten? The longest stint I'd ever done in solitude was a month. It was only on the third day, when I was near delusional from lack of drink, that she deigned to instruct a servant to deliver a pitcher of water and a pittance of bread.

Rain tapped at the darkened panes and the moon rose like a summoning as I fretted a worry line into the wood of the floor with my continuous to-and-fro. I didn't mind the solitude so much as I wondered whether this was to be my fate until my proposed wedding day, leaving me no opportunity to see Ilona again. I worried my fingers in my skirts until a madcap notion sprouted from the spores of desperation seeded in my mind.

The window latches needed little persuasion to open. The squeal of the neglected hinges was covered by a god's blessed growl of thunder as I nudged them wider. I peered over the sill at a wisteria-covered lattice and grinned. I had an escape.

Shucking my slippers, I slunk out the window, tentatively testing my weight on the crosshatched beams and woody vines. They held firm as I made my descent by the light of the moon peeking through the navy clouds trimmed by its pearly luminescence. The wisteria petals caught in my hair, their perfume and the freedom I felt as my stocking-covered toes struck sodden ground was heady and intoxicating. I hiked my skirts and darted for the tree line to skulk and dash in the inky shadows toward the lapping music of water striking the ground.

The hemlock and rushes brushed my cheeks in welcome as I crawled into my hollow. They tangled behind me, locking me in as though they knew I needed to feel the protection of their embrace at my back. The rain misted over the ethereal chop of small waves, and a moonbow blossomed darkly, arching over the top like the entry to another world. And perhaps it was. Maybe if I could swim out to it, the prismatic jewel tones would feel as solid as marble beneath my fingers, and I would be able to pass through a veil to wherever it was my sidhe came from, and she and I could—

A splash interrupted my musings, and suddenly Ilona was there watching me from behind a cluster of pink lilies.

Her eyes latched onto me like two inky buttons as she drifted soundlessly through the waves in such a way that made me realize the slight sloshes that she made were simply a kindness to alert me to her presence.

"Hello again, woman of mud"—she paused, clicking her tongue thoughtfully against her serrated teeth—"Lucrecia." Ilona trilled my name as if it were a musical note. The sound of it fluttered like the ruffling of an owl's wing inside my chest.

"Good evening." My words slipped as soft as silt from my tongue, and I blushed. My thoughts had eddied around her, never fully able to sweep past daydreams of seeing her again since the first moment she'd plinked the golden pendant back onto the stone. My gaze drifted between her dappled green breasts to where it hung, and the flush on my face deepened.

Ilona rested her cheek on the bend of my knee where I had them crossed before me. The rest of her lithe body drifted behind her, floating just below the surface. "What brings you to my pond tonight, Lucrecia? Do you have more pretties you wish to toss away?"

I laughed and shook my head, stray wisps of hair stuck to my cheeks from where they'd flown free of the coronet my hair had been painstakingly braided into that morning. "I'm sorry, Ilona, I don't have any pretties for you tonight. I simply wanted . . ." How could I explain my predicament to such a wild thing? It would have been like trying to explain the confines of a cage to a bird who'd only known the openness of the sky.

A wash of dizziness swept over me, and I wobbled where I sat as the world seemed to tilt on its axis. When was it last that I had eaten? I must have eaten breakfast . . . but no. My stomach had been a tangle of knots, so it must have been the morning last before the party. I pressed a finger to my lips as nausea took the place of dizziness.

"You are unwell?" Ilona raised her head, and though she had no brows, her forehead furrowed all the same. She levered herself up and sat down on the stone next to me. There was barely enough room, so the profiles of our bodies had to press against one another. She was surprisingly warm. It was not the warmth of a human body but of a swim in sun-warmed waters.

"I-I'm hungry is all," I managed to stammer as my words stumbled over my thundering heart that was far too excited about our proximity.

Ilona hummed in disapproval. "You will wait," she demanded as she reached up and stroked a hair off my cheek and twirled it around one of her long fingers.

I felt that touch echo across my skin as she slunk back into the waters and disappeared, leaving me ensorcelled and alone. I raised a hand and pressed it to my cheek as if I could prevent the misting rain from wiping the evidence of her touch from my flesh.

I was unaware of how much time had passed. I would have waited, rooted in that spot, until I was nothing more than a pile of bones just because she asked it of me. I let my eyes drift shut, and I let the sounds of this haven I'd found fill me until a slight disturbance in the air around me told me she'd returned.

Ilona climbed onto the bank, crossed her legs, mimicking my position, and motioned for me to face her so our knees touched. In her lap, she held a fragment of log covered in a variety of aquatic delicacies. She plucked what looked like a slivered chunk of some sort of mushroom off her makeshift platter and pressed it to the seam of my lips. "Eat," she demanded in a melodic and rasped tone that told me there would be no refusing her even if I wished to. She could have asked me to drown myself, and I would have filled my pockets with stones gladly.

The gilly-frilled flesh of the shroom was meaty. It tasted of loam and woods, as if I were eating the very essence of the ecosystem I was shrouded in. I moaned into the morsel, savoring each squish of inky juice as I chewed. Ilona smiled and proudly fed me a pinch of green leaves, mint, next.

In silence, she gave me the tender and savory scraps she'd scavenged—dandelion root, cress, flower petals, and slivers of raw fish—until I no longer felt weak from the hunger and instead felt bold.

"Here." I picked up a plump pink piece of fish and offered it to her. "It's only fair that we share this feast."

She leaned forward and closed her lips around my offering. Her tongue twined around my fingers, and her teeth scraped against me, ever so gently, as I withdrew. I shuddered as an ache blossomed like a lotus between my hips. She chewed, each gnash of her perfect teeth slow and deliberate, with her eerily entrancing bulbous eyes fixated on mine until she swallowed.

We leaned in toward each other, sharing air that felt as charged and as wild as the atmosphere before a lightning storm, and I wondered if I pressed my lips to hers whether it would be as ecstatically beautiful as the blue bolts that cut through tumultuous skies. And then suddenly I didn't have to wonder; she was tasting me and I her. The spill of her hair slipped like algae through my fingers as we tangled tongues stained with the juices of mushrooms and moaned into one another.

Ilona straddled me, the damp of her sinuous body pressed against me, and pinned me to the rock as she deepened the kiss. It felt feral and freeing. It loosed something deep within me that had sat tethered and silent. She trapped my lower lip between those lethally beautiful teeth of hers and dragged me deeper into her thrall. My hands roamed the curves and swells of her burnished skin, claiming every inch of her until we at last pulled apart panting. Her dappled skin glistened gray and green in the slivers of moonlight that peered at us between rolling clouds. No, not moonlight. Those were the first rays of the sun, peeking its sleepy eyes over the distant horizon.

"Time for you to go, Lucrecia," Ilona purred as she slunk off my lap and back into her watery home.

I struggled to sit up, breathless, for she'd stolen all the air in my lungs with those kisses. "Wait," I whispered after her as she sunk slowly into the ripples. She paused, her hair sweeping over her shoulder as she cocked her head to the side curiously. "Can we . . ." I didn't know how to finish that question. Instead, my words trailed off, falling and sinking like two pitifully cast pebbles into the pond.

But she knew what I meant without saying it, I could tell in the sheen of her endless eyes as she tipped her head. "Come see me again, anytime. I will be waiting for you." And then she was gone.

On steps so light I felt as though I had wings, I flew back along the lawn as dawn spilled pink across it, up the trellis, and over my sill where I shucked my muddied clothes and slipped beneath my sheets. Despite the fluttering excitement that pattered against my heart, I fell asleep in an instant and dreamed I had webbing between my fingers and Ilona's

lips pressed against mine beneath the
silvery waters.

CHAPTER THREE

The door to my chamber banged open with an ear-splitting crack as the knob ricocheted against the wall, and I jolted from a heady and intoxicating dream that left me feeling wet between the thighs. My mother charged in, and for a horrifying moment, I thought perhaps she knew about my rendezvous with the sidhe in the pond, but then I saw her face. It was contorted into a strange shape, one I'd not seen on it often, one that almost looked—elated. And that, well, that was quite frankly the most terrifying sight.

"Up, up, up!" she demanded, honking like a mother goose chiding her goslings. "We have much to do today." A swarm of maids with bolts of white, ivory, and cream fabrics, laces, and ribbons streamed into the room like a mess of bees let loose from their hive.

I drew the coverlet up around my bare chest, shrinking back against the pillows and away from the unfamiliar eyes of all the women. Grandam bustled in, lagging behind the rest with a tray containing a single steaming kettle and a cup and placed it on the bedside table. She smiled at me softly as she poured me some weak tea without honey or cream. So it would appear I was still being punished then. I took a sip and winced as the scalding liquid seared its way down my throat. "What exactly is it that we're doing, Mother?"

She cast a peeved glance over her shoulder at me, her lips twitching down in annoyance. "What does it look like, Lucrecia? We're having you fitted for your wedding gown."

I choked, tea spraying across my bed set. "Already—but it is not for months yet."

Her expression soured further, like milk left too long in the pail. "Yes, well, the timeline has changed. Tursel has decided he would like to be wed right away. Tomorrow in fact."

"To-tomorrow?" My whispered word tripped over my trembling lip, and my gaze flicked dazedly to the pond and back to my mother again.

Her features softened, and she sighed in a way that I would have called dreamy were it any other person, but from her, the sound was simply confounding. "Lord Tursel will arrive for the wedding tea in the morning. The priest will marry you at noon, and you'll be on your way to his manor before sundown." She spun round as if struck with an afterthought. "You will have to consummate the marriage. You do know what that entails, yes?"

Giggles echoed around the room from maid to maid like a contagion. "Silence!" my mother demanded, and they all hushed. "Well, do I need to explain it to you, or are you well enough informed? I won't have this family embarrassed if you cannot provide an heir for your husband."

I swallowed hard around dread that felt more like a choking fist than a simple lump in my throat and nodded. That seemed to mollify her well enough to leave me be while she continued to direct the help. I'd seen a man and a woman rutting before in the woods, and I had to say it did not impress. The idea of that man atop me in such a way stirred a violent nausea to life in my stomach. But then I looked out the window to my little silvern haven and was suddenly awash in the flush of memories from last night so vivid if I closed my eyes, I could still feel her dewy skin beneath my fingertips, and a whole host of butterflies split from their cocoons to riot in my ribcage. I raked my teeth over my lower lip, lightly swollen from our stolen hours, and sighed before I resigned myself to my mother's clutches.

The rest of the day was spent being primped, pinned, poked, prodded, and swathed in silks until my mother was satisfied and I was trussed up like a bride, or a confection fit for devouring.

As dusk began to claw its way across the sky, dragging with it clinging storms, worms of dread wriggled in my belly and slunk their way into my brain. What would become of me if I could no longer seek solace in Ilona? I closed my eyes, painted with shimmering pearlescent powders, and tried to imagine being in

Tursel's embrace, but the notion felt clawed and talon-tipped in my mind. I stood mute as my mother and maids drifted out of my chambers, satisfied that they'd molded me into an acceptably meek bride, but in my soul, I screamed. When at last the door was shut and the lock slid into place, I flung myself onto my bed and sobbed.

It took much longer for the house to grow still save for the scurrying of mice and the plink of rain on the windows than it had the night before. But as soon as the cacophony dulled, and I was certain all were abed, I made my way back to the pond's edge, left on the precipice of my sanity, my lip worried between my teeth.

Ilona was already there waiting for me, her chin resting on our rock next to a thoughtfully prepared feast arranged in a riot of pinks and greens atop a bark platter. I spilled across the stone, no longer able to contain my anguish as soon as I saw her. My sobs tore through my chest, and tears flowed freely down my flushed cheeks. Ilona raised herself out of the water just enough to gather me in her damp arms. I melted into the curvature of her, letting her draw my legs around her hips. My feet and calves slipped into the welcoming waters, and I rested my head on her shoulder. She soothed a webbed hand over my sodden hair, still perfumed with the oils my mother had me anointed in, as she hummed a melody that ebbed and flowed in harmony with the songs of nature that surrounded us. "There, there, my mud girl. Do not fret. Whatever it is that is bothering you, we can fix."

I hiccuped against her sweet loamy-smelling skin as she swayed me to the beat of the lapping waters and the bellow of frogs. "I don't know that we can . . . I am trapped in a spider's web, and the creature is set to descend on the morrow." I shuddered as Ilona trailed her fingers along the ridges of my spine, only a flimsy and soaked layer of diaphanous fabric between her skin and mine. "I can feel his fangs on me already."

A growl reverberated in Ilona's chest. The vibration of it pressed itself into my bones and made the endings of my nerves quiver. Her fingers, which had only been moments ago been gentle, dug into the swell of my hip and thigh possessively. "This spider cannot have you, Lucrecia, not if you are mine." Her words and her grip made me quiver, and on impulse, I pressed a kiss along the curve of her swanlike neck. Her skin was soft and slick and tasted delicious. She was decadent and forbidden, and the notion of being hers, of being claimed by her, sent a heat ravaging through me that burned like a summer brush fire and torched all other thoughts.

She arched to give me more room to leave a trail of kisses along her tender skin, and her growls turned into contented moans as I slid my lips and dragged my tongue across every inch of her collarbone and down her sternum. Emboldened by her panted breaths, I swirled my tongue around a peaked nipple and relished the sound she made as I scraped my blunt teeth along it. Slithering her fingers through my hair, she fisted the strands and pulled my head back with a hiss. "Be still, my woman of mud. I am to lay claim to you tonight, not the other way around. There will be time for that later."

Oh the sweet promise of later. It was like a drug, heady and intoxicating, and for the first time, I understood what it was that people chased after in one another. Her long fingers slipped to the hem of my shift and danced beneath it until she found the embroidered ribbons that neatly tied my stockings. She plucked their ends like leaves from a vine, peeled them from my legs inch by tantalizing inch, and tossed them into the pond where they floated for a moment like the specters of who I once was before they sank into a watery grave.

She slipped back beneath my bunched-up skirt, her touch dancing higher and higher, until at last the cool press of her slick skin met with the sodden and heated petals that blossomed at my core. I gasped, and she swallowed the sound with her mouth, drinking it in like a bee at a flower sucking down nectar as she stroked me from the inside out, filling me with her webbed fingers. I was a storm cloud, and she was a god summoning lightning, building it up within my depths until I was so full of it I wanted to shatter into a thousand luminous pieces. She let her mouth wander, let me sing my pleasure into the night, becoming one with the riotous hymns sung by the pond and all those that lived in it. Her teeth—those glorious, serrated teeth—grazed, snagging my sensitive taut skin through my shift, and I was unleashed. As a torrential downpour of ecstasy struck, rippling through me, I broke around her.

Ilona picked up the pieces of me, put them back together, and cradled me in her arms, pulling me out into the water with her. We drifted, our fingers entwined, among the lilies, suspended together for what might as well have been eternity for all the peace and contentment I felt from it. But the sun would soon rise and break our spell, and so with great reluctance, I splashed back to our stone.

My monster, my maiden who'd somehow managed to consume me heart and body and soul in such a short time, leaned in as I tried to rake my fingers through my hair to disentangle the wreath of decaying leaves that had found their way into my locks as we'd swum together. "Now that you are mine, I will show you how to rid yourself of your pests." She whispered her sidhe wisdom into my ear, her breath hot and alluring, tempting me to sink between her thighs to mimic what she'd done for me. But then she pressed the lacy white bouquet of flowers, plucked from the pond's edges, tied togeth-er with the gilded chain and pendant that brought us to one another, into my hands and a kiss to my lips. She bid me farewell, for now, for the last time. Because after today, she promised we need never to part again.

CHAPTER FOUR

I was waiting perched like a bird on the swing of its cage for my mother to come. I'd already dressed in my gown, pinned my hair, and painted my face, making sure there was no trace of the night left on my skin. She froze as she entered, and I could see the panic grip and twist her features as her gaze fell immediately to my empty bed. She thought I'd run. I knew better. If I were to simply run, she would have me hunted down, and if she didn't, Lord Tursel certainly would have. That vile spark in his eyes held a hunger too deep and raw and raging in their merciless depths for him to simply let me fade into the mist without a second thought. No, this was the only way.

The moment my mother saw me, her expression softened into one of relief, and for a teetering moment, I wished that it was because I was safe and unharmed and not because I was now a representation of the wealth she would soon have. But I knew better than to let that notion root like an invasive weed. There was only one creature that had claimed me, that I knew loved me, and it was not the woman who'd birthed me.

"You gave me a fright child, lurking there in the shadows." Mother gasped. Her free hand fluttered to her heart while the other fisted the cloth of my bridal cloak, her knuckles whitening and pinking again.

"I'm sorry." I whispered the words meekly and dipped my head in contrition. She crossed the room in a few short strides, and I stood as she shook out the folds of elaborately embroidered cloth. She settled the thing over me, concealing the ivory underneath. It was meant to be an ill omen should the groom see the bride's dress before the ceremony. A silly superstition. I was going to bring misfortune to him should he see my skirts or not. The green of the fabric reminded me of Ilona's skin, and a smile tugged at the corners of my lips as I recalled how it felt to slide my fingers along her flesh.

My mother mistook my expression, as she cinched the ribbons along the front of the vestments shut. "You seem to be warming to the idea of marriage. I must admit I was worried you might do something rash after your little display of hysterics."

"Yes, Mother. I am eager for the day's end." And the end of this charade.

My father coughed from where he stood in the threshold. "Time to go, Lord Tursel's carriage has just arrived. We'd better hurry this along, funds won't be transferring into our accounts until the ink on the marriage contract is dry, and I'd very much like to head into town to celebrate this evening. I've meetings to attend, you know." He looked down his nose at me, sweeping his gaze up and down, then up once more, but never quite high enough to meet my eyes. No, he wouldn't want to humanize the daughter being sold to the highest bidder like chattel.

Without another word, we proceeded from the room and down the hall, the only thing keeping me steady and sure of foot as I marched like a convict to the gallows was the steady and reassuring press of the golden orb against my clavicle. It was no longer a symbol that I was possessed by him. The musky scent of the flowers pressed into it tickled my nose, and my smile deepened. No, now it was a symbol of my freedom and of

my love for the strange-eyed beauty
in the pond who'd claimed me.

The slip of the clasp and the plink of
the filigree necklace into the bottom
of the teapot sounded as loud as a
parade in the too-silent room from
where I stood, completing the ritual
of marital tea service. As was tradi-
tion, the bride-to-be was to start her
marriage with an act of servitude and
submission to her betrothed by making him a pot of tea. With my back to
the room, and my parents doing their
best to keep Lord Tursel contented,

nobody seemed to notice the extra clink of metal in the porcelain pot.

Hurriedly, I shoveled other herbs into the brew—lavender, rose petals, calendula—all strong flavors to hopefully mask the taste of the flowers pressed tightly into the center of the gilded pendant. I leaned over the mouth of the teapot and took a tentative sniff as I poured scalding water over the flora. The wafting steam smelled like a delightful summer bouquet with no warning hint of what lurked beneath the benign.

Satisfied my poison was undetectable, I did as Ilona instructed, stirring the concoction thrice backward before whispering the phrase she gave me in a tone so hushed I wasn't even certain I spoke aloud. The language of the spell was unfamiliar and clumsy on my tongue, but it also tasted of her, so I savored each word as I willed it to work as she said it would, increasing the potency of the plant's toxins tenfold.

"Are you growing the tea herbs yourself?" Tursel mocked in a smarmy, teasing tone that thinly veiled his deprecation of me. "Are you quite finished yet?" My parents tittered at his jibes at my expense, and I felt a flush creep up my neck, but not one of embarrassment. Rather, one of rage.

"Yes, I'm coming, only a moment more," I called back over my shoulder as I settled the lid back atop the pot. With careful hands, I cradled the tea, avoiding the belly of the kettle so as not to scald my fingers as I walked softly to the table.

Deftly, I poured the brew into my betrothed's cup, offering him honey or cream, of which he took neither, before moving next to my father and mother. I poured a serving for myself last before taking my seat beside Ignatius. I made a show of dallying—arranging my skirts, stirring a dollop of honey into my cup, and a heavy-handed pouring of cream. Not that any of them noticed, as they nattered on to one another between sips.

After a few moments, Ignatius coughed, the sound hard and firmly lodged in his throat. "I beg pardon," he rasped, "but what in the blazes did you put in this?"

Across the way, my father was beginning to sweat, fat beads rolling down his temples and the bridge of his nose. My mother made a sound halfway between a wretch and a gag. I smiled, pinning the saccharine expression on before replying, "Nothing special, a bit of lavender, rose, you know the usual. Oh and a bit of hemlock."

"You fool woman, don't you know that's poison?" He sputtered as he threw the cup off the table. As if that could save him now. The painted pottery shattered beautifully against the floor.

I tsked. "You underestimate me even now, my lord. Of course I know it's poison, why else would I have put it in there?"

My mother's skin went waxy, and she spewed across the table. Convulsions set in all around, and all three of their bodies slipped from their chairs with a satisfying crash.The cakes on the table looked divine, shaped like roses with pink cream frosting, and so I sampled one as I watched and waited for the poisonous hex to take effect. As soon as I saw the graying of Tursel's fingers, I knew my will had been done.

I stood, fished my necklace from the teapot, shed my cloak, and stood over my betrothed's writhing body. Our gazes locked as his veins turned dark, and I fastened the bauble back around my neck, a bit of pretty petal peeking out from between the golden whorls. His eyes bulged as he watched me stroke a finger down the chain. "I remembered my necklace today," I said sweetly, before hiking my skirts and striding out of the room.

Grandmother stood in the hall, her face a wretched mask of horror. She flinched when our gazes locked and she spotted my honeyed smile. But even that could not peel the glee from my cheeks. "Do not worry, Grandam, they aren't dead. They have simply been made to reflect on the outside what they were made of on the inside, cold stone. And it won't be forever, like all curses, true love's kiss will set them free. Though you might have a blessedly hard time finding someone who truly loves *them*." I laughed as I pressed a kiss to her withered cheek before dancing joyously on my way.

By the time I made it to the front door, my shoes were shed, and I broke into a run.

The dew-damp grass tickled the pads of my feet as I flew across them for the edge of the pond. I tore through the thicket of hemlock and dove into the pool, not stopping to wait on our stone as I'd done before. The water rushed up to wrap me in its embrace. It saturated each thread of my wedding gown and dragged me down to where my beauty waited below the surface with her wicked smile. We came together in a clash of lips and limbs before we swam hand in hand for a luminous glow in the distant depths of the silvern waters. It wrapped us in ribbons of light, and everywhere it touched me I changed, metamorphosing into something marvelous and new, something more like her, my Ilona.

When we surfaced on the other side of the ardent bubble of light, the world too was changed. Gone was the simple pond. Spread before us was a crystalline lake teeming with unfamiliar flora, the sky was the succulent pink of sunset, and the wind smelled sweet against my dewy skin, and I understood that my monster and I were at last home.

The End

THANK YOU
FOR READING

Beneath The Silvern Pond came to me randomly one day while I was intending to just do a writing exercise. It was of course an eerie, rainy day, so it was extra dark in my basement office, aka the perfect atmosphere for writing. So, I made a cup of spicy chai, lit my favorite candle and put a fresh piece of paper in my Royal and let the words bleed onto the page. The story surprised me, and spooked me just a little (yes, I scare easily) and I loved it immediately.

This was a hard year for writing for me; I spent much of the first half of the year editing The Seventh Sister and wondering if anything I ever wrote was worth a damn or if I should throw in the towel entirely. But writing Ilona and Lucrecia got me through some of the nastier bouts of imposter syndrome and for that they will always hold a special place in my heart— my maiden and my monster.

And now for the part where I thank everyone who has been in my corner. This book would have never come to fruition without the support of so many. First, my chosen sister, my work wife, Cynthia, who is always there for me and pushes me to keep going when things are dark. I also couldn't have done it without my feral heart worm Jenn, your reader reactions and your hype and your friendship feed my soul. As always thank you to Heather for being my forever beta reader from the time I was twelve and spouting story ideas to you on hikes to now. Thank you so much to Steph, I'm so grateful that you always make time to alpha or beta or to listen to my random voice notes.

As always, a special thanks to my husband for supporting my dreams even before I thought I could pursue them and for being my real life book boyfriend. To my kids who even now are putting up with me being on the computer for more hours than I should and for still thinking it's cool that I write books. Thank you to my mom for supporting my love of reading which turned into a love of writing and for coming with me to the worst book convention ever— well go to a good one together someday.

To my editors, Beth and Chrissy, thank you for making my mad ramblings readable. Without you there would be so many plot holes, too many commas and an embarrassing amount of spelling errors.

And last but never least, as always thank you God for gifting me with the many worlds and stories that revolve in my head that I get to put on the page.

Pennies Worth of Dread

Beyond The Iron Gate

Beneath The Silvern Pond

Below The Loam (Coming 2026)

The Strattaria Chronicles

The Seventh Sister

The Travelers Series

The Songs That Beckon

Echo Across the Sands

Whispers From The Fade (Coming

Soon)

The Gods Fall Series

Illuminator of Dreams (coming 2026)

www.ingramcontent.com/pod-product-compliance
Lightning Source LLC
Chambersburg PA
CBHW050424110726

47899CB00008B/2836